Dog and Bear

TWO FRIENDS · THREE STORIES

Laura Vaccaro Seeger

A NEAL PORTER BOOK
ROARING BROOK PRESS
New York

To my mother, Vera,
and
my mother-in-law, Marge,
with love and admiration

A Neal Porter Book

Published by Roaring Brook Press

Roaring Brook Press is a division of Holtzbrinck Publishing Holdings Limited Partnership

175 Fifth Avenue, New York, New York 10010

Distributed in Canada by H. B. Fenn and Company, Ltd.

Library of Congress Cataloging-in-Publication Data

Seeger, Laura Vaccaro.

Dog and Bear / by Laura Vaccaro Seeger. — 1st ed.

v. cm.

"A Neal Porter Book"

Summary: Three easy-to-read stories reveal the close friendship between Dog and Bear.

Contents: Bear in the chair—Play with me! Play with me!—Dog changes his name.

ISBN-13: 978-1-59643-053-2   ISBN-10: 1-59643-053-2

[1. Best friends—Fiction.   2. Friendship—Fiction.   3. Dogs—Fiction.   4. Bears—Fiction.]   I. Title.

PZ7.S4514Dog 2007   [E]—dc22   2006011687

Roaring Brook Press books are available for special promotions and premiums.

For details, contact: Director of Special Markets, Holtzbrinck Publishers.

Printed in China

First edition March 2007

10 9 8 7 6 5 4

"is that you, Bear?"

"Yes,
Dog."

"It is a beautiful day," said Dog.
"Come outside with me."

"I can't get down," said Bear.

"Just jump."

"But I am scared!"

"Come closer. You can slide down my back."

"You can do it," said Dog.
Bear was more frightened than ever.

Dog said, "Take one step. One little, tiny step."

"Now, take one more."

With each step, Bear became braver. Finally, Bear reached Dog.

"Whee! That was fun!"

"Good. Now we can go out," said Dog.
"Where is your scarf?"

"Uh-oh," said Bear.

"Maybe we should just stay inside," said Dog.

"Bear, will you play
with me?"

"Not right now, Dog.
I am reading my book."

"Please, Bear. Play with me."

"I am reading a story about a dog
and a stuffed bear."

"Oh, Bear. Play with me!"

"In this book, the dog
and the bear are
best friends."

"Come on, Bear.
Play with me!"

"Although they love to be together,
sometimes the bear just needs
time to himself," said Bear.

"Play with me! Play with me!"

"Play with me! Play with me!"

"The bear tried to explain this to the dog,
but the dog did not understand," Bear continued.

"Play with me!
Play with me!"

"After a while, the bear realized
that the dog just wanted
to be with his friend," said Bear.

"All right, Dog. I will play
with you now. What shall we do?"

"Read to me! Read to me!"

"I am changing my name," said DOG.

"But why, DOG?"

"Because DOG is b-o-r-i-n-g!
From now on, call me SPOT."

"But you don't have any spots."

"What about FLUFFY?" said DOG.

"You are not fluffy."

"SKIPPY?"

Bear smiled.

"ZIPPY?"

Bear thought
for a moment.

"HOW about **MY BEST FRIEND DOG?**" said Bear.

"I like that!" said DOG.
"Or just DOG for short!"

"Perfect," said Bear.